A Paw Island Christmas

Written by:

Corey Maxwell

Illustrated by:

Paul Turnbaugh
Steve Vitale

Original Music Composed by:

Mark Hladish, Sr.

Recorded by:

Mark Hladish Productions

Walworth, WI USA

Be an Islander!

Visit our website at

www.pawisland.com

Library of Congress Catalog Card Number: 99-96021

Paw Island Entertainment, Inc.

709 W. Main Street, Lake Geneva, Wisconsin 53147

This Paw Island Musical Belongs to:

____

Date:

____

♩♪ Paw Island Theme ♫♩

Narrator: Christmas is a special time on Paw Island. But for most islanders, there was one Christmas that was far better than any other. That was the Christmas it snowed.

It all started one day when Kee Kat and Allie were out exploring like they do and came across Buford Wagley decorating his Bait Shack.

Kee Kat: Hiya, Buford! Whatcha doin'?

Buford: Why hello Kee Kat! I'm decoratin' for Christmas.

Kee Kat: Decoratin'? Pawesome! But, what's all that white stuff?

Buford: Oh, them's cotton balls. They're supposed to be snow.

BAIT

Kee Kat: Snow? What's that?

Buford: Oh, jumpin' crickets, I keep forgettin' some of you all ain't never seen snow before. Guess it's too hot around here. Anyhoo, snow's just one of the things that makes Christmas special.

Kee Kat: Nuh-uh! Only presents do that!

Allie: (in kittenspeak) <Yeah>

Buford: Oh my, have a seat little critters, and I'll tell you a story. You see, when I was just a pup back in the Land of People, why, I used to think the same as you. Mm-hmm. Shoot, to me, Christmas was all about...

Kee Kat: Hey, hey, hey Buford, did the human people ever talk about snow?

Buford: Why, yes, they did. Mattera fact, I used to hear all kinds of humans talkin' about snow. Just seemed kinda cold and wet to me, but, oh them humans sure did like it. They even had songs about it. But like I was saying…

Kee Kat: They had songs about SNOW?

Buford: Yep. Sure did. But like I was sayin', Christmas is...

Kee Kat: Oh! Oh! Oh! Sing one Buford! Sing one!

Buford: Well, leapin' tadpoles, I ain't sure I remember any songs nowadays, it's been so long...

Kee Kat: Oh, oh, oh! Please sing a song about snow Buford!

Buford: I don't rightly recall many...

Kee Kat: I'm sure you know the words!

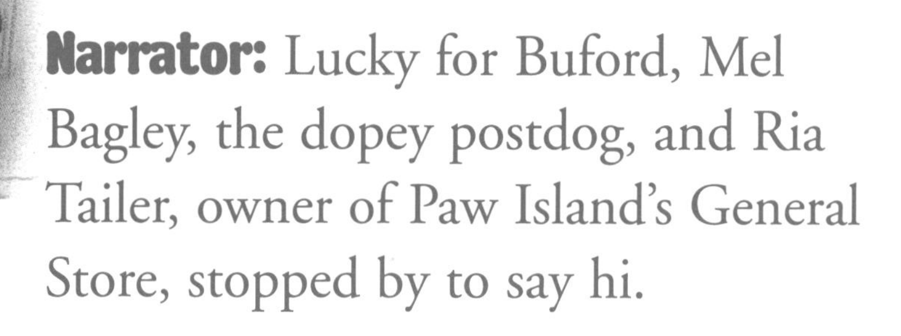

Narrator: Lucky for Buford, Mel Bagley, the dopey postdog, and Ria Tailer, owner of Paw Island's General Store, stopped by to say hi.

Mel: Hey everybody, what's going on?

Kee Kat: Buford's gonna sing a song about snow!

Mel: I know some of them songs—like that "Floppy the Snowman" and...

Ria: "Floppy the Snowman?" Oh, Mel!

Mel: Well, how about maybe that "Jiggy Bells" one then...

Kee Kat: Hey, can anyone sing a song about snow?

Ria: Well, I'm sure we could probably cook something up, couldn't we boys?

♩♪ **When The Snow Falls Down** ♫♩

Kee Kat: Wow! This snow thing sounds Pawesome! Can you really make snowmen with it?

Ria: Oh yes...and you can make snowballs and snowforts…

Buford: And snow tunnels…

Mel: And snow cones...

Kee Kat: Wow! I think I'm gonna ask Santa for snow this Christmas! That's the one present I want. No other presents for me! Just snow, snow, snow, and more snow. Snowbidy doe. Snow, snow, snow!

Dear Santa

Buford: Oh my, the little critters just don't understand Christmas yet, do they?

Mel: Nope.

Ria: Not quite yet!

Narrator: That night, Kee Kat wrote his wish list to Santa Claus. And from top to bottom, the only thing on his list was snow.

♩♪ **Dear Santa** ♫♩

Narrator: But alas, it looked like Kee Kat's wish would not come true. Day after day he awoke, ran outside, and found nothing but green grass and brown dirt. But then, the night before Christmas, something amazing happened! For the first time in the history of Paw Island, it started to snow. When Kee Kat awoke the next morning, he was surprised at what he found.

Kee Kat: I bet it didn't snow aga... WOW!!! Yipee!! Snow!! Oooh!! Oh, it's COLD!! And scrunchy! Weeee!!! Snow!

Narrator: All morning long Kee Kat played in the snow. He made snowdogs and snowcats, and snow forts and snow tunnels. He threw snowballs at Butch and made snow angels with Fifi. But by the afternoon, he was wet and cold. He shivered and sniffled, and soon decided to visit Buford so he could dry his fur and warm his paws.

P.I.F.D.

Kee Kat: H-h-hey B-b-buford, I-I-I thought you s-s-said s-s-snow for Christmas was a g-g-good thing!

Buford: Why, snow is good, Kee Kat. Just depends on how you look at things, I reckon.

Kee Kat: Well, I don't like it. I'm cold, and I wish I would have asked for a different present!

Captain Nick O'Time: Attention! Attention! I have a special announcement!

Buford: Hey, do you hear that? Somethin's goin' on outside.

Captain Nick O'Time: Mayor Graham Paw has declared an island emergency. Everybody is to meet at Whisker Winds Resort until the storm passes! And hurry! We don't want to lose anyone in the snow.

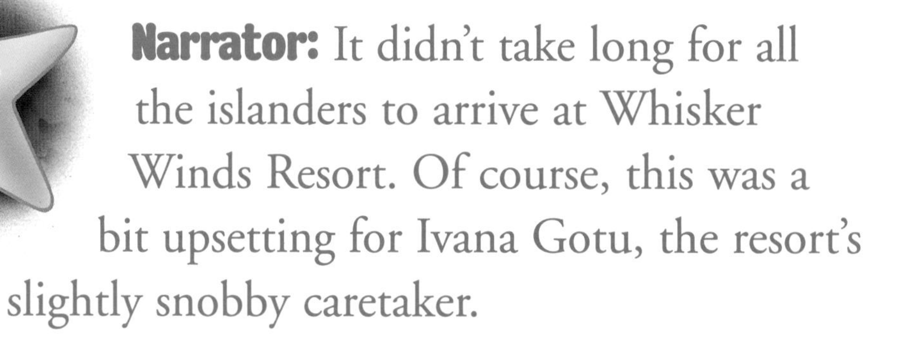

Narrator: It didn't take long for all the islanders to arrive at Whisker Winds Resort. Of course, this was a bit upsetting for Ivana Gotu, the resort's slightly snobby caretaker.

Ivana: Oh my, my, my, my, my! Please all of you, do be careful. Butch, that chandelier is NOT a jungle gym...do get down! REALLY! Oh, you there, wipe those paws...I just had that rug cleaned...

Graham Paw: Attention! Everyone, attention! Excuse me! There. That's much better...we can hear ourselves think.

Mel: I don't hear a doggone thing!

Everyone: Shhhhh!

Ivana: Oh, I do hope this dreadful storm ends soon—we really must find a more CIVILIZED way to pass the time.

Kee Kat: I know, let's all sing Christmas songs!

Graham Paw: Ah, now that is a splendid idea, Kee Kat!

Narrator: Everyone agreed, and, after just a bit of confusion over the words...

Mel: I swear it was "Jiggy Bells" where I came from!

Narrator: ...they all started to sing.

Butch: Hey, let's sing that "Here Comes Santa Claus!"

Ria: How about "Santa Claus is Comin' to Town?"

Mel: Hey, I got an idea, let's sing "Who Got the Red Hosed Rain Gear!"

Everyone: Mel!

Mel: What did I say?

Buford: It's supposed to be "Rudolph the Red Nosed Reindeer!"

Mel: Oh, I'm sorry.

Narrator: And so it went, on into the night. As the snow continued to fall, dogs and cats continued to sing. Islanders who hadn't seen each other all year exchanged hugs, while others met new friends. Even the biggest sourpusses managed to get along with others—if only for an evening.

Ivana: I heard that!

Narrator: The snow brought everyone together and taught Kee Kat a valuable lesson. As he listened to the songs and the laughter, he realized that Christmas is about more than getting presents. He learned that it's about caring. And sharing. He learned that it's about giving and forgiving...and spending time together with friends and loved ones. And, in the end, it's about the way everyone should live their lives—every day and in every way.

Everybody: MERRY CHRISTMAS EVERYONE!!

♩♩♪ Everyone Loves A Holiday ♫♩

VOICES

Narrator: Fred Brennan

Kee Kat: Pam Turlow

Buford Wagley: Gary Joy

Allie: Pam Turlow

Mel Bagley: Mark Hladish, Sr.

Ria Tailer: Nancy Potter

Nick O'Time: Corey Maxwell

Graham Paw: Gary Joy

Ivana Gotu: Pam Turlow

Butch: Mark Hladish, Jr.

SONGS PERFORMED

Paw Island Theme
Mark Hladish, Sr., Kim Weiss

When the Snow Falls Down
Gary Joy, Mark Hladish, Sr.,
Nancy Potter, Jeanette O'Dierno

Dear Santa
Pam Turlow

Jingle Bells
Mark Hladish, Sr., Gary Joy,
Nancy Potter, Lanie Kreppenneck,
Mark Hladish, Jr.

Everyone Loves a Holiday
Mark Hladish, Sr., Kim Weiss

Graphic Design: Utopia, Marengo, IL

Paw Island Theme

I know a place where the sun shines
every day
(Paw Island)
Sail on a breeze and chase all your
troubles away
(Paw Island)
Every day begins, a celebration with
your friends
The adventure never ends at Paw Island.

Imagine a place where the sky is
bluer than blue
(Paw Island)
And all of your island friends are
waiting for you
(Paw Island)
Playing in the sun, there's room
for everyone
So come and join the fun at Paw Island.

(Paw Island)
Come to a place where the sun shines
(Paw Island)
Imagine the sea and a blue sky
Come on everyone, to Paw Island!

When the Snow Falls Down

Buford: In the fall the leaves turn brown.
Mel: The wind blows and they float to the ground.
Ria: The weather's changin' and rearrangin'
the town.

Mel: There's a chill in the winter breeze.
Ria: And all the ponds and the streams
start to freeze.
Buford: And soon you can bet that the
snow will be falling down.

Lead and Background vocals:
It's winter and the snow is falling.
Let's all make a snowman!
Can't you hear old man winter calling you?

Buford: Grab your friends and let's go sledding
Mel: Hey, I say let's go man.
Buford, Mel, Ria: When the snow is falling,
there's so many things you can do.

Mel: When the snow falls down, down, down
Background vocals: When the snow falls down

Mel: When the snow falls down, down, down
Background vocals: When the snow falls down

Ria: Let's make a pile of snow on the ground.
Buford: And move our arms and legs up and down.
Mel: And make the shape of an angel in the snow.

Buford: Or make snowballs and throw 'em
at a tree.
Mel: Hey, Buford, don't throw that snow at me.
I don't like it when I get snow up my nose.

Lead and Background vocals:
It's winter and the snow is falling.
Let's all make a snowman!
Can't you hear old man winter calling you?

Buford: Some folks like cross country skiing.
Mel: Hey! There's another snow sport.
Buford, Mel, Ria: When the snow is falling,
there's so many things you can do.

Mel: When the snow falls down, down, down
Background vocals: When the snow falls down

Mel: When the snow falls down, down, down
Background vocals: When the snow falls down.

Dear Santa

Dear Santa, I'm writing you this letter,
I hope it gets to you.
I had the kitten pox, but now I'm feeling better,
I hope that you are feeling okay too.

Because Christmas day is coming and everyone is counting on you.

Dear Santa, I've tried to be a good boy,
I wanted you to know,
This Christmas, I'd trade in all my new toys,
If you could find a way to make it snow.

And I know that it's a big thing to ask someone to do,
But Christmas day is coming and everyone is counting on you.

Santa Claus, I'm counting on you.

Jingle Bells

Dashing through the snow, in a one horse open sleigh
O'er the fields we go, laughing all the way!
Bells on bobtails ring, making spirits bright,
What fun it is to laugh and sing a sleighing song tonight.

Oh, jingle bells, jingle bells, jingle all the way.
Oh what fun it is to ride in a one horse open sleigh
Jingle bells, jingle bells, jingle all the way.
Oh what fun it is to ride in a one horse open sleigh.

Mel:
I love Christmas cake, and I love Christmas turkey
I love Christmas pie, and I love Christmas jerky.
I love Christmas cookies, and I love Christmas punch
I love Christmas dressing…
Hey, ain't it time for lunch?

Oh, jingle bells, jingle bells, jingle all the way.
Oh what fun it is to ride in a one horse open sleigh
Jingle bells, jingle bells, jingle all the way.
Oh what fun it is to ride in a one horse open sleigh.

Everyone Loves a Holiday

Little one, dream of all the fun
That a Christmas day can be
Close your eyes, dream of starry skies,
And a snowy Christmas Eve.

Dream of laughing and singing,
Dream of Christmas bells ringing...

Because everyone loves a holiday,
Everyone loves a holiday
Everyone loves a Christmas dream come true.

Girls and Boys dream of special toys
Underneath the tree
Mistletoe, carols in the snow,
And a happy memory.

Dream of loving and caring,
Dream of giving and sharing...

Because everyone loves a holiday,
Everyone loves a holiday
Everyone loves a Christmas dream come true.

Everyone loves a holiday
Everyone loves a holiday
Everyone loves a Christmas dream come true.

Everyone loves a holiday
Everyone loves a holiday
Everyone loves a Christmas dream come true.

Everyone loves a holiday
Everyone loves a holiday
Everyone loves a Christmas dream come true.

Everyone loves a holiday
Everyone loves a holiday
Everyone loves a Christmas dream come true.

Everyone loves a holiday
Everyone loves a holiday
Everyone loves a Christmas dream come true.

Kids, see if you can find the hidden smiley faces!

There are two smiley faces hidden in every illustration. See if you can find them all. If you can, then you are truly a great detective.

Need a Hint?

See below…there is one hint for each hidden smiley.

Page 1: Keep your eyes on Buford's basket. The blades of grass around the Shack are worth looking at.
Page 4: See the bushes above Allie's head. What do you turn to open the door?
Page 5: The trunk of the far left tree holds a secret. See the dirt around Kee Kat's shadow.
Page 8: Green plants are great. See the shingles above the door.
Page 9: Smile back at the middle tree trunk. See the tree above Mel's head.
Page 12: Look closely at the candle plate. Is that wheel smiling at you?
Page 13: The snowflakes hold both secrets. See the bushes next to Kee Kat. Then look straight down from Kee Kat's right foot.
Page 16: The door is open! See Kee Kat's blanket.
Page 17: Look real close at all the wreaths. Check out the bulbs around the room.
Page 20: Keep your eyes on the bottom of Graham Paw's podium. One of the bows knows.
Page 21: Oh Christmas tree, oh Christmas tree! Look real close at the upper right ceiling rafter.
Page 24: Look closely at the snowflakes on the lower left corner of the building. See the small bush to the right of the building.
Page 25: Look at the lonely bulb. The tuft of Graham Paw's hat seems real happy.